From one Cool Cat to another,

—The Cat in the Hat

Movie Storybook

Adapted by Justine & Ron Fontes

Based on the motion picture screenplay written
by Alec Berg & David Mandel & Jeff Schaffer

Based on the book by Dr. Seuss

RANDOM HOUSE 🏠 NEW YORK

www.randomhouse.com/seussville   www.universalstudios.com
www.catinthehat.com

ISBN: 0-375-82869-9

Printed in the United States of America   First Edition   10 9 8 7 6 5 4 3 2 1
RANDOM HOUSE and colophon are registered trademarks of Random House, Inc.

Any place, any time,

Anywhere, any town,

A Saturday in summer

Is the best day around.

You could swing swings, kick kickballs,

Scoot scooters down Main.

You **COULD** have done that . . .

. . . But it started to rain.

The rain kept young Conrad and Sally Walden inside, where Conrad was doing what he did best—making trouble! Conrad's newest stunt nearly splattered Mom's party dress with mud.

"Why did you have to pick *today* to destroy the house?" Mom wondered as she came in the door.

"I told him Mom's throwing a very important party," Sally said. "But he went right ahead—wrecked the house and let Nevins get away."

That boy is always headed for trouble! Diver Dan and I would never do anything as crazy as surf down the stairs.

What was Mom to do? Conrad was a boy who did the opposite of what he was told, and Sally was a tattletale.

Just then, there was a knock on the door.

It was the next-door neighbor, Mr. Quinn. He was holding Nevins, the Waldens' dog. "I found him in my yard," Quinn said.

Mom sighed. "Thanks, Lawrence. You're a saint."

Quinn flashed his sparkling smile. "And I thought you were just dating me for my good looks."

While Mom got ready for the party, Quinn pestered her about sending Conrad to military school. "The Wilhelm Academy made me the successful senior V.P. of sales and compassionate human being you see before you," he said proudly.

Even Nevins rolled his eyes.

"Do you mean the military school for troubled youth?" she asked. "I'm not sure that's right for Conrad."

"You're going to love it," Quinn said to Conrad as Mom left the room. "It's like summer camp, but with soul-crushing discipline."

Conrad and Nevins were sure of one thing: Quinn was no saint.

Suddenly, the caterer arrived with heaping trays of food. But Sally had other plans for the kitchen. She consulted her PDA and informed Mom, "Two weeks ago you said today was good for making cupcakes. See?"

"No, honey. The party's tonight," said Mom. "I'll take you to a friend's house if you want to make cupcakes."

But Sally wouldn't hear of it. "Last time, Ginny wanted to be head chef, Denise talked back to me, and Eileen was too bossy," said Sally. "I won't tolerate it."

"Right, well, I guess you'll both be staying home," Mom said. "Since Conrad is grounded."

Conrad and Sally were both yelling at Mom when the phone rang.

"Quiet!" Mom yelled at the phone. But when she finally answered it, she did not feel one bit better.

Sally is a great kid when it comes to rules. Too bad you can't order people to be your friend, or schedule a smile.

An important client named Mr. Filene was in town just for the day. "I have to show him some houses," said Mom. "I hope Mrs. Kwan can baby-sit."

While they waited for Mrs. Kwan to make her way up the drive, Mom reminded the children of The Rules. "No playing ball in the house, no fighting, no answering the phone 'city morgue,' no touching the party food, no messing up the house, and absolutely no one sets foot in the living room, or else . . ."

"Or else you'll send me to military school?" Conrad asked.

That made Mom really upset. "If you behaved, I wouldn't have to consider it. I wish I could trust you." Then she took Conrad's Game Boy and stormed out the door.

The kids slumped in their chairs,
Too glum to complain.
And to make matters worse,
It continued to rain.

They could stare out the window,
Or perhaps get a nap in,
And hope that something—
Anything!—might happen.

And it did! As Mrs. Kwan snored
and Conrad tapped the fishbowl—*BUMP!*—
something rather large thumped upstairs.
"What was that?" Sally wondered.
Who—or *what*—had arrived?

Kids, don't turn the page. It's too scary!

Slowly, the children crept upstairs, where they saw something that just could not be! Conrad gasped, "It looks like a humongous cat!"

The Cat popped up right beside him. "I prefer the term 'big-boned' or 'jolly.'"

"Aiiighhh!!!" cried Conrad and Sally, diving under the bed.

"No. Ka-aaaaaat!" the Cat said. But no matter where the children hid, the giant Cat was there.

Once the children had stopped screaming and hiding, the Cat presented his card. "I'm the Cat in the Hat. There's no doubt about that! Nice spread you got here," he said, running down to the living room. He sat right on top of the snoozing Mrs. Kwan. "What a lumpy couch!"

"That's our baby-sitter!" yelled Sally and Conrad.

"Baby-sitter? You don't *really* need one of those, do you?" the Cat asked. Then he hung Mrs. Kwan up in the closet like an old sweater.

And with a full musical accompaniment from a CD inside his hat, the Cat began to sing. . . .

"I know it is wet
And the sun is not sunny,
But we can have lots of good fun
That is funny."

"You can juggle work and play!
But you have to know the way.
You can keep afloat a wish,
Like the way I do this Fish.
You can be a happy fella.
Someone throw me that umbrella.
And that fan,
And that toy man . . ."

As he sang, the Cat started balancing more and more things. Then, just as he reached a high note, the Cat belched—*BURP!*—and everything tumbled toward the floor—even the poor Fish in his bowl. The kids watched in horror. But somehow, the Cat caught each item, except the Fish, who flopped into the teakettle. *Kersploosh!*

"Listen to me, children, this Cat should not be here when your mother is not," the Fish warned.

But the children were far too excited to listen. "That was wicked cool!" Conrad exclaimed.

"Do it again!" Sally added.

"Shamu is right. I really should be going," said the Cat.

"No! Don't go!" begged Conrad.

"All right, I'll stay," said the Cat. "But first, you need to sign this contract. Basically, this guarantees that you have all the fun you want and nothing bad will happen."

That sounded good to Conrad and official to Sally, so they signed away.

Then the Cat strolled into the living room. With Conrad's skateboard and a drill and jack from his hat, he turned the couches into trampolines, *just like that.* BOING! The Cat was doing the most amazingly fun flips. "I could use some company," he called to the kids.

Conrad dove onto the couch and started to bounce. This *was* fun that was funny!

Sally hesitated.

"Be strong," said the Fish. "You don't need to bounce around like a monkey to have fun."

But before the Fish could finish . . .
Aiiieeeee! Sally was bouncing high into the air.
"It's like being in the circus!" she exclaimed.

Conrad agreed. "And the best thing is,
no one will ever . . ."

Just then, the door opened. It was
Quinn.

". . . find out," finished Conrad quietly.

When my mother told me rules,
I listened, and fish don't even have ears!
But Conrad and Sally, well, you'll see.

"Oh, Mr. Quinn. I was just telling Conrad to get off the couch," Sally fibbed.

Mr. Quinn growled in a voice Sally had never heard before. "No one likes a tattletale." Then he ate a sandwich from Mom's party tray and revealed his plan. "One more mistake and Conrad's in military school," said Quinn. He turned to Sally. "Then it will just be me, your mom, and *you*—cooking and cleaning."

As the evil neighbor rattled on, the Cat clung to the ceiling out of Quinn's view. Quinn suddenly sneezed. *ACHOO!* "Is there a cat in here? I'm allergic to cats."

"No, no cats," Conrad said, even as the Cat sent a cloud of fur flying toward Mr. Quinn.

The Fish tried to get Quinn's attention. "Hey! He's right above you. Look up!"

But Quinn was too busy sneezing.

The Cat dangled Diver Dan in front of the Fish. "One more peep out of you and Diver Dan loses his air supply." Then he flung the frightened Fish into the toilet bowl.

Oh my Cod! That's where they buried my brother.

ACHOO! Quinn couldn't stand another sneeze and ran out the door.

"That was amazing!" yelled Conrad.

"We totally got away with it!" shouted Sally.

"So, what shall we do next?" asked the Cat.

"I want to make cupcakes!" yelled Sally.

Suddenly, the Cat was hosting his own TV cooking show. "Do you love making cupcakes, but hate all the hard cupcake work? Say hello to the amazing Kupkake-inator." The Cat held up a weird gadget. "This delightful device instantly makes cupcakes out of anything you have in the kitchen."

"Anything?" the Cat asked himself.

"Yes, anything!" the Cat answered, grabbing everything that wasn't nailed down and throwing it into the Kupkake-inator. Then the Cat opened his umbrella and—*KABOOM!*—the oven exploded in a volcano of purple goo!

"Cat, you need to clean this up, pronto!" Sally said. "We have a contract."

The Cat started mopping up the goo with a large towel.

"That's no towel! That's Mom's party dress!" shouted Conrad and Sally.

"You've ruined it!" Sally cried.

"Oh, what will become of us? Your mother will lose her business. And we'll have to live on the street!" the Fish fretted. "I can take care of myself, but what about Diver Dan?"

"I'll take care of everything," said the Cat, and he dashed outside.

The Cat came back dragging a large wooden crate. "Put your hands together for the answer to all your cleaning needs," he announced. "In this box are two Things. I will show them to you. Two Things, and I call them Thing One and Thing Two!"

Twin mop-topped creatures bounced out of the crate, chattering like squirrels chasing each other around a tree.

"Nippa deepa depp," jabbered Thing One.

"Delippa dikka bapp," yelped Thing Two.

Thing Two wanted to be called Thing One and Thing One wanted Thing Two to get over it. While the Cat tried to make peace between the quarreling Things, Conrad lifted the lid of the crate. Something bright and bristling with energy seethed inside.

SLAM! The Cat shut the crate. "This isn't just any old crate," the Cat said. "This is the Trans-Dimensional Transportolator—the doorway from this world to mine. I'm not a big rules guy, but this is my one: Do NOT open the crate! No lookee, no touchee! Got it?" said the Cat, putting a lock on the lid.

Conrad nodded. But as soon as he was alone with the crate, he tickled the funny crab lock until it popped open. To his amazement, the lock scrambled off the crate and onto Nevins!

Before Conrad could get a good look inside the crate, the Cat, Sally, and the Things came back in the room with Mom's purple-stained dress.

Each Thing grabbed one end and they snapped the dress tight. The purple spot flew off the dress and landed on the couch! *SPLAT!*

"That's not helping!" said Sally.

So the Things beat the couch with tennis rackets till the spot sprang onto the drapes.

"Dear sweet mother of Cod!" the Fish gasped. "They're wrecking the whole house!"

And indeed the Things were running wild, up the walls and onto the ceiling, in a purple parade of filthy, unfettered fun.

The Fish tried to call Mom for help. "Who is this?" she demanded.

The Fish answered, "It's someone you know. Someone who watches you all day, sitting in dirty water. . . ."

Mom hung up!

Silly air-breathers! Think they're so smart because they have telephones and hands. But what good is a phone if the person you're calling for help won't listen?

The Things were chasing each other and the children were chasing the Things when the Cat asked Conrad, "Do you know what happened to the lock on this crate?"

"No, and I'm a little busy!" Conrad shouted.

But when the Cat looked him in the eyes, Conrad finally confessed. "Okay, I was curious. I was going to lock it up again. But now it's on Nevins's collar."

Just then, Sally cried, "They have Nevins!"

The Things started throwing the little dog like a football.

"Stop throwing him!" Sally shouted. But those Things just tossed Nevins some more.

"Why do they always do the opposite of what you say? That's so annoying," Conrad said.

That gave Sally an idea. "Hey, Things, *don't* let go of that dog!"

It worked! The Things let go of Nevins, but now he was headed toward the open window.

"Catch him!" Conrad yelled. Realizing his mistake, he shouted, "I mean, *don't* catch him!" But it was too late. Nevins sailed out the window and scampered across the street.

Sally grumbled, "The house is destroyed. The party is ruined. And now Nevins is gone."

"That's nothing compared to what's going to happen if we don't lock this crate," the Cat added. "It's already leaking."

Purple tentacles oozed out of the crate. Everything they touched sprang to strange, squirming life.

Conrad and Sally tried to shut the crate, but the powerful purple goo pushed the lid open again. "It won't stay shut without the lock," the Cat explained. "If we don't get that lock off Nevins and back on the crate, this house will soon be the Mother of All Messes."

"We have to go out there and find Nevins," Conrad declared.

"Impossible!" the Fish exclaimed. "Sally, you're not allowed to leave the house without an adult, and Conrad, you're grounded."

But, as usual, no one listened to the Fish. Instead, they used Mrs. Kwan to weigh down the crate and headed out into the day. The Cat left Thing One and Thing Two to take the children's place at home.

"See!" said the Cat. "It's too nice to stay indoors."

To the kids' surprise, the dreary day was suddenly sunny.

Meanwhile, next door, Mr. Quinn was watching TV and making telephone sales calls. His couch was covered in overdue bills. Quinn was hardly the "successful senior V.P." he pretended to be. In fact, three brawny brutes from Safari Sam's Big-Screen Jungle had come to take back his TV.

Quinn searched his pockets. "How about if I give you three dollars and twenty-eight cents, and a coupon for ten tacos?"

But the brutes wheeled the TV out in the middle of a show. *Blink!*

Quinn sulked in his chair, then smiled and headed for his car. He could get thirty tacos with his remaining money.

Ooh, that Quinn makes my fins crawl!

The kids and the Cat soon spotted Nevins. But the Cat scared the dog, who ran right through a neighbor's birthday party.

Sally gasped. "Denise? Ginny? Eileen? Everyone I know is here. Why didn't Denise invite me?"

"Maybe because you told her never to speak to you again," Conrad reminded her. "Don't worry about it. Let's just get Nevins and go."

But before they could get away, the birthday party suddenly was moved outside to the yard. Sally and Conrad hid, but the Cat had nowhere to go.

It was time to hit the piñata. But that was no piñata—that was the Cat. Just as the party guests noticed the giant Cat, Conrad thought fast. He threw handfuls of the only thing in the world that could make the children forget what they saw— candy!

They still had to catch Nevins. But unfortunately, Quinn caught Nevins first on his way back from the Taco Shack. He grabbed the little dog and drove off with him. "Joan will be steamed when she finds out Conrad lost the dog again. Bon voyage, Private Conrad."

"We're doomed," Conrad said.

"What's he going to do with Nevins?" Sally cried.

"Be strong," the Fish said. "Oh, what's the use? All is lost! Whatever can we do?"

Okay, so I panicked. You would, too.

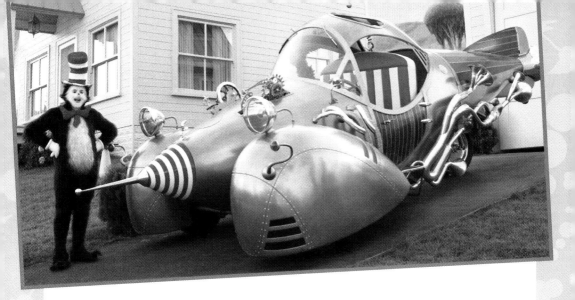

The Cat pulled an automatic garage-door opener from his hat. "Why don't we take my car?" A garage suddenly appeared. Inside was the strangest car the kids and the Fish had ever seen—the Super Luxurious Omnidirectional Whatcha-majigger, or S.L.O.W., for short. "Buckle up," said the Cat. "We're on a mission!"

"Red light. Red light!" cried the Fish.

"Not for long." The Cat squirted green paint on the light and proceeded to drive through the busy intersection. Brakes squealed. Cars swerved. Conrad and Sally screamed.

The Fish freaked out! "Do you even have a driver's license? I *refuse* to let you drive!"

"You're right!" said the Cat. So he slid the steering wheel over to Conrad's side of the car. S.L.O.W. slowly slowed down. "Use your imagination! Make the car noise," the Cat said.

"*VRRRRROOOOMMM!*" said Conrad, and S.L.O.W. lurched forward full speed. Conrad was driving. "This is awesome!" he shouted.

"I want to drive," cried Sally.

"Two people can't drive!" said the Fish.

"Right again!" said the Cat. "*Everyone* should drive." The Cat pressed a button and a steering wheel popped up in front of Sally, himself, and even the Fish.

Kids, please don't try this at home!

"One-way street!" the Fish screamed.

"Not for long." The Cat squirted the DO NOT ENTER sign with green paint. But that didn't make the street any wider or stop the truck that was barreling toward them.

"Truck!" Sally screamed.

"Truck!" Conrad yelled.

"Hey, Rhode Island license plate. You never see those," observed the Cat.

Everyone turned their wheels and S.L.O.W. bounced up onto the curb and spun out of control. *SMASH!*

Conrad stumbled from the wreckage, dazed but deliriously happy. "Can we do that again?"

The Fish was as white as baked flounder. "I think I wet my jar."

The Cat said, "Great parking space! Now let's go find that unpleasant pet of yours."

They quickly spotted Nevins with Quinn. The nasty neighbor was heading into a store.

Quinn tied Nevins up, then went inside.

Conrad untied Nevins, who was very glad to see the kids. But before they could get away, Quinn came out. The kids and the Cat bolted.

"Come back here, you little maggots!" Quinn shouted.

"I've got it!" said the Fish. "We'll give ourselves up and admit to everything."

Conrad took the lock off Nevins's collar. Sally checked her PDA. "If we go home right now, we can lock the crate, clean the house, and have four minutes and eighteen seconds of unstructured playtime before Mom gets home."

But just then, Conrad looked across the street. There was Mom's office—and Quinn was getting into Mom's car with her!

"Cat, we've got to get home before they do. Do something!" Conrad exclaimed.

But the Cat just shrugged his shoulders.

"It's all my fault. Why do I always do the opposite of what I'm told?" Conrad moaned . . . and that gave him an idea.

"That's it. The opposite!" Conrad shouted, "Things, DON'T help us. DO NOT help us get home right now!"

HONK! Things One and Two suddenly drove up in Quinn's car.

"Get in!" Conrad yelled.

Now you're thinking, Conrad!

So they all squished into Quinn's sporty vehicle. But were they too late? The Cat panicked. "Game over, man! That crate's been open all day. The house is going to be the Mother of All Messes, and your mom's going to be home any second! Look at the PDA. We don't have enough time!"

Sally tossed the contraption out the window. "Forget the PDA. Step on it, Conrad. We can *do* this!"

Conrad said, "Hey, Things, DO NOT do anything to slow down my mom."

So, of course, that's just what they did. Pretending to be motorcycle police, the Things pulled Mom over to give her a ticket. Quinn grabbed their motorcycle and sped off.

When the kids, the Cat, the Fish, and Nevins got home, Quinn was waiting for them outside. "When I finish telling your mom all you've been up to today, there'll be *two* new cadets in the family," Quinn growled.

But when he made the mistake of walking into the Walden house, which was indeed the Mother of All Messes . . .

I wouldn't go in there!

. . . Quinn fell off an impossibly steep cliff, vanishing into the clouds below.

"How do we find the crate?" Sally wondered.

"We follow the mess back to its source," Conrad replied.

Mrs. Kwan floated by, a snoring log adrift on the purple river of weirdness. "Hop on," the Cat said. And they rode Mrs. Kwan down the stair rapids and through the wildest house anyone could ever imagine.

In the DVD version, you can see the outtakes where they fall off Mrs. Kwan and everyone gets soaked in purple goo.

"That was great!" said the Cat. "Let's ride the Kwan again."

Sally scowled at the Cat, then shouted, "There's the crate!"

Conrad and Sally were really steamed. But it was their own fault. I told them that Cat was trouble.

Conrad, Sally, and the Cat forced the crate shut. *FLOOSH!* All the weirdness shrank and swirled into a brilliant cloud and was sucked back into the crate! Conrad snapped the crab lock back on.

"I did it!" the Cat exclaimed. Then, when he saw the looks on Conrad's and Sally's faces, he added, "Okay, *we* did it."

Sally looked around. Sure, there weren't any more giant mountains or purple rivers, but the house was a disaster, every inch an absolute mess!

The Cat asked, "What game should we play next? Tennis, anyone?" Then he pulled some tennis rackets out of his hat.

"You didn't help us, and now you want to play?" Sally asked.

The Cat grinned. "Yep! And wasn't that a lot more fun? You guys did great. Though I was afraid you'd catch the Things before they threw Nevins out the window."

Sally could hardly believe her ears. "You knew they would do that?"

"Of course. I planned the whole day!" the Cat purred. "I even got your mom out of the house."

"No," Sally said. "She had an appointment with Mr. Filene."

"It's pronounced FEE-line," the Cat corrected.

Conrad gasped. "That was *you*? And you even knew I'd open the crate?"

"Why do you think I made it my one rule? I knew you couldn't resist," the Cat explained. "Now how about that game of tennis?"

"Game? The house is destroyed! You said nothing bad would happen," Conrad said.

"Yeah, we had a contract," Sally added.

The Cat pulled out the contract and showed them the fine print. "The contract will be null and void if Conrad chooses to open the crate and loses the lock."

"Get out!" Conrad said coldly.

"I don't know that game," the Cat said.

"It's not a game. None of this is a game," Conrad replied.

"Cat, you need to go," Sally agreed.

Finally, the Cat grabbed his crate and left.

"I'll get the mop and bucket," Sally sighed. "Conrad, you may want to get out of here until Mom calms down."

Conrad shook his head. "This was all my fault. Why don't you go upstairs?"

"I'm staying with you," Sally said. "We should share the blame." She took her brother's hand.

Conrad smiled. "Thanks, Sal."

Then the door swung open. The kids braced for a furious Mom, but it was the Cat riding an amazing machine. He showed them more fine print in the contract. "If Sally and Conrad learn from their mistakes, the contract shall be reinstated." Then he added, "Now let's play one last game called Clean Up the House. Kids, meet the Dynamic Industrial Renovating Tractormajigger."

Conrad and Sally said, "D.I.R.T.?"

"That's right," the Cat said. "Nothing cleans better than D.I.R.T.!"

The Things had their own mini-cleaning machines, too.

I knew the Cat would come back! I knew he'd help us.

In a flash and a song, the house was cleaner than clean from the drapes to the fishbowl. Even Mrs. Kwan was cleaned of purple goo. The Cat and the Things went out the back door just as Mom came in the front. "All right, kids, this place had better not be a mess, or I'm . . ." Mom could not believe her eyes.

Mrs. Kwan jumped off the couch, wide awake. "Ms. Walden, home so soon? The children were angels."

But when Mom walked Mrs. Kwan to the door, there was Quinn, covered in goo and looking like a train wreck. "Lawrence, what happened to you?" Mom asked.

"Your demon children!" Quinn raved. "They destroyed your entire house. . . . I fell off a cliff, and there was a giant cat and . . ."

"Who? Lawrence, you're not making any sense," said Mom.

"You better straighten yourself out or you'll never find a job," said Conrad.

"Joan, you can't believe him. You know what kind of kid your son is," Quinn countered.

Mom said, "Yes, I do. Conrad can be irresponsible, he makes bad choices, and sometimes he makes me want to tear out my hair. But he's a good kid and I believe in him. Now I'd like you to leave."

Quinn fell on his knees and begged, "Joan, marry me."

But Mom just slammed the door in his face.

Mom's party was a big success, and so were Sally's cupcakes. All of Sally's friends thought they were delicious.

"What did you put in them?" Mom asked.

"You can make cupcakes out of anything," Sally said. Then she and Conrad burst into giggles.

Mom eyed her children curiously. "Just what *did* you kids do today?"

Well, what would *you* say if your mother asked *you*?

The family was whole,
All thanks to the Cat,
Who was dashing and charming,
No doubt about that.

Trust him to take all the credit. At least he cleaned my fish tank and dear old Diver Dan.